Ted Prior

Grug

For Dougal, Lucy and Eve

GRUG LEARNS TO SWIM

Published in Australia and New Zealand in 2009 by Simon & Schuster (Australia) Pty Limited
Suite 19a, Level 1, Building C, 450 Miller Street Cammeray NSW 2062

A CBS Company
Sydney · New York · London · Toronto · New Delhi

Visit our website at www.simonandschuster.com.au

National Library of Australia Cataloguing-in-Publication entry

Author:	Prior, Ted.
Title:	Grug learns to swim / Ted Prior.
ISBN:	9780731813995 (pbk.)
Series:	Prior, Ted. Grug.
Target Audience:	For children.
Dewey Number:	A823.3

Cover and internal design: Xou Creative
Printed in China: Asia Pacific Offset Ltd

The paper used to produce this book is a natural, recyclable product made from wood grown in sustainable plantation forests. The manufacturing processes conform to the environmental regulations in the country of origin.

9 8 7

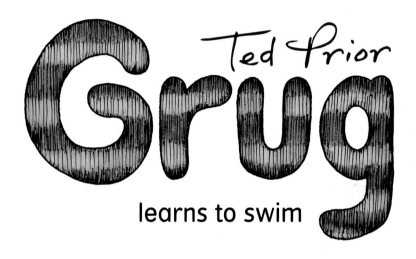

Ted Prior

Grug

learns to swim

SIMON & SCHUSTER
AUSTRALIA
A CBS COMPANY

Grug felt happy. It was a clear sunny day – a fine day for a walk.

He strolled down to the creek.

Grug found Cara the carpet snake
sleeping on a rock in the sun.

Cara awoke …

… and she slid gracefully into the water.

Grug plunged in after her …

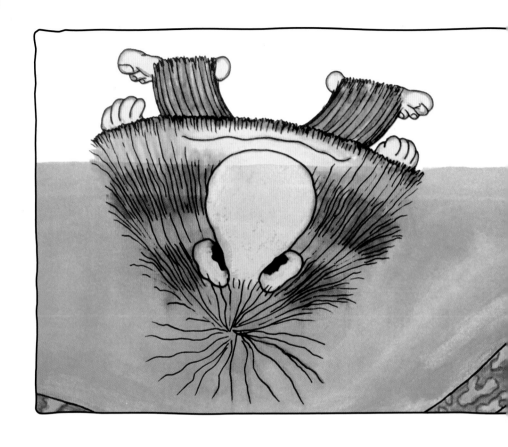

... but he could not swim!

Cara dragged sorry, soggy Grug
up onto the grassy bank.

Grug would have to learn to swim.

Grug slowly, carefully, walked into the water.

To his surprise he floated ...

… the right way up!

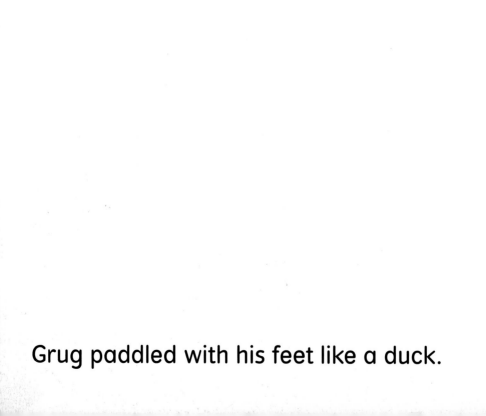

Grug paddled with his feet like a duck.

At last, Grug could swim!

Grug

Grug at
the beach

Grug and his
bicycle

Grug and the
big red apple

Grug builds
a boat

Grug builds
a car

Grug and his
garden

Grug goes
fishing

Grug goes
to school

Grug and the
green paint

Grug has a
birthday

Grug and
his kite

Grug learns
to cook

Grug learns
to dance

Grug learns
to swim

Grug meets
Snoot

Grug and
his music

Grug in the
playground

Grug plays
cricket

Grug plays
soccer

Grug and the
rainbow

Grug goes
shopping

Grug at
the snow

Grug at
the zoo